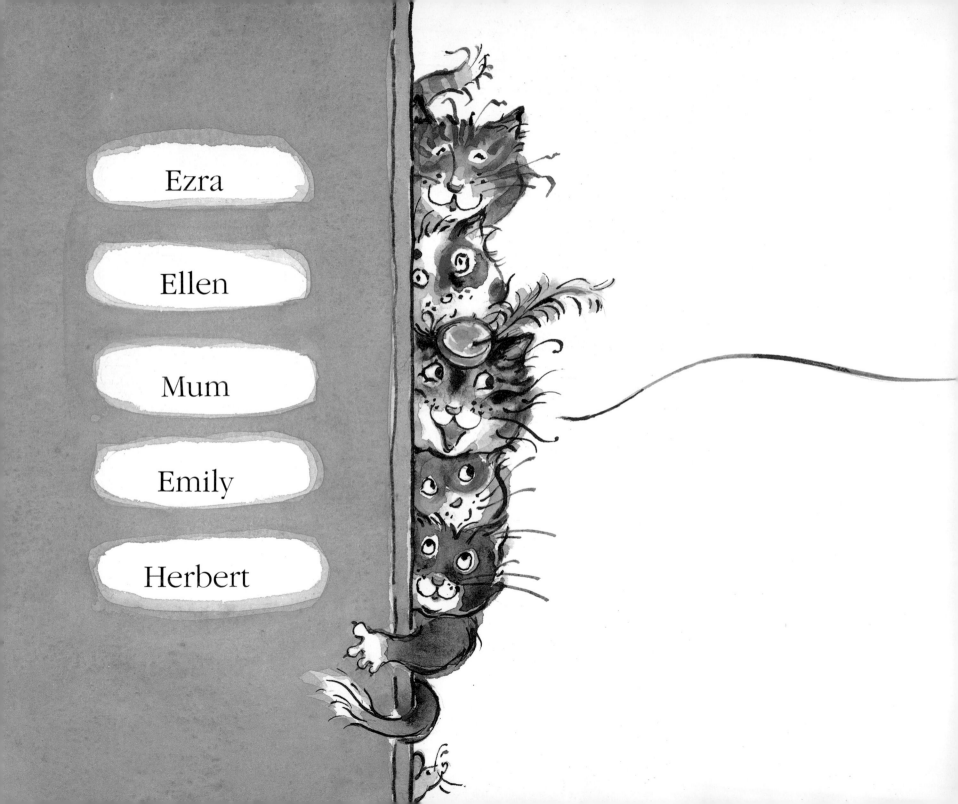

Ezra

Ellen

Mum

Emily

Herbert

Back Soon

Diana Hendry

with pictures by

Carol Thompson

RED FOX

For Julie, with love, Diana
For Maureen and the boys, Carol

A Red Fox Book

Published by Random House Children's Books
20 Vauxhall Bridge Road, London SW1V 2SA

A division of Random House UK Ltd
London Melbourne Sydney Auckland
Johannesburg and agencies throughout the world

Copyright text © Diana Hendry 1993
Copyright illustrations © Carol Thompson 1993

1 3 5 7 9 10 8 6 4 2

First published in Great Britain by Julia MacRae 1993

Red Fox edition 1999

Printed in Singapore

RANDOM HOUSE UK Limited Reg. No. 954009

ISBN 0 091 87296 0

There was only one thing wrong with
Herbert's mother. Sometimes she would
go out without him. Whenever she did,
she always said the same thing.
"Back soon!" she said and gave
him a loving cuff on the ear
with her paw.

"Back soon!" she said when she went down to the corner shop for something she had forgotten. She left Uncle Ezra to look after him and she was back in five minutes.

"Back soon!" she said when she went to have her whiskers curled at the whisker dressers and was gone for hours and Big Sister Emily looked after him and wouldn't play Chase-the-Cotton-Reel.

"Back soon!" she said when she went into town to buy herself a new dress and was gone the whole day and bossy Aunt Ellen made him eat all his mouse-tails.

And "Back soon!" she said when she and his father, Enoch, went off for a whole weekend to see distant relations. They said they needed a holiday. Aunt Ellen, Uncle Ezra and Big Sister Emily all looked after him.

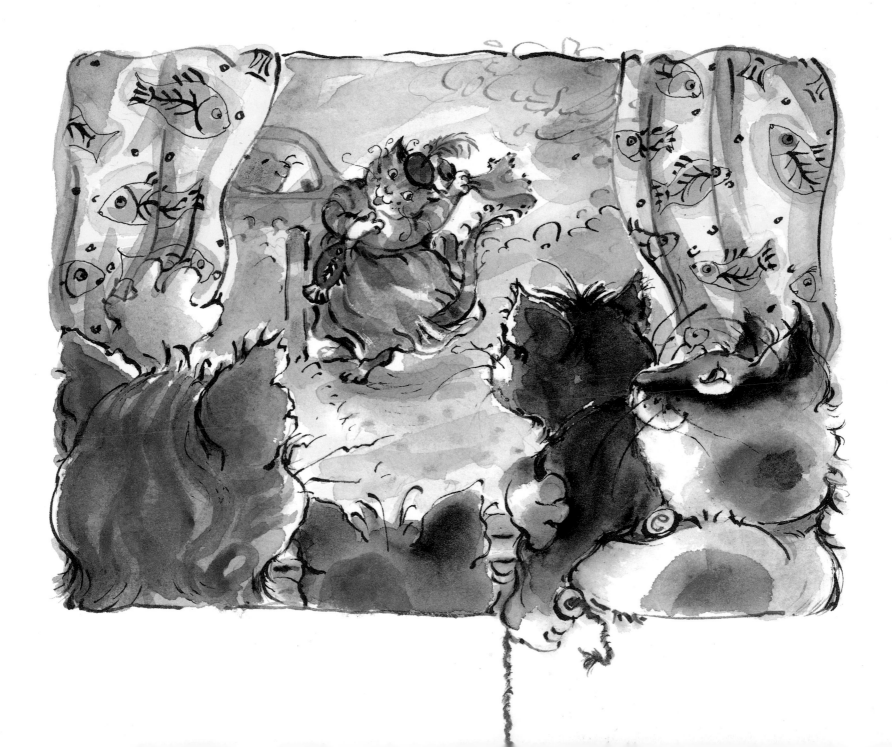

One day Herbert decided it was *his* turn. When his mother was ironing the pillow cases, Herbert said, "I'm going under the table now. Back soon!"

Herbert stayed under the table for a whole five minutes. His mother carried on ironing. She didn't seem to miss him at all.

Back soon

Herbert tried again. "I'm going up to my room now," he said. "Back soon!" His mother was cooking supper. "Don't be long," she said. "Supper's nearly ready."

Herbert stayed in his room for ten whole minutes twiddling his paws. It was very boring. When he came downstairs, his mother said, "You're just in time. Supper's ready."

The next morning it was sunny and windy. "I'm going out into the garden," said Herbert very loftily to his mother. And over his shoulder, when he reached the kitchen door, "Back soon!"

It was so nice in the garden that Herbert quite forgot he had said he would be back soon. He played being an acrobat on a branch of the lilac tree. Then he chased a stick that kept running away from him. He was just making himself nicely dizzy chasing his own tail when he heard a very sad voice coming from the open kitchen door.

"Oh where is my Herbert?" cried this voice. "He said he'd be back soon and he's been gone for hours and I'm very lonely and I miss him terribly!"

Herbert stopped chasing his tail, steadied himself up and ran into the kitchen and into his mother's arms. "I'm back! I'm back!" he cried. "Did you miss me?"

"Oh I really did!" said his mother. "But it's quite nice having some time to yourself, isn't it?"

"It is," agreed Herbert, "as long as you always remember to come back."
"I always will," said his mother.
"So will I," said Herbert.